Merry

Christmas on Dewberry Lane

Book Five

Cheryl Wright

Copyright

MERRY

(Christmas on Dewberry Lane Book Five)

Copyright ©2021 by Cheryl Wright

Cover Artist: Black Widow Books

Editing: Amber Downey

Dedication

To Margaret Tanner, my very dear friend and fellow author, for her enduring encouragement and friendship.

To Alan, my husband of over forty-six years, who has been a relentless supporter of my writing and dreams for many years.

To Virginia McKevitt, cover artist and friend, who always creates the most amazing covers for my books.

To You, my wonderful readers, who encourage me to continue writing these stories. It is such a joy knowing so many of you enjoy reading my stories as much as I love writing them for you.

Table of Contents

Chapter One

Dewberry, Montana – 1880s

Merry Jensen brushed the hair back off her face. It had already been a long day and was far from over. It wasn't often like that at her diner, *Ma's Kitchen*, named after her mother, who had died some time ago.

Ma had taught Merry everything she knew about cooking and baking, and it had helped keep the only diner on Dewberry Lane afloat. So did the stagecoach that came through Dewberry every week. Luckily for Merry, the stage office was located on the same block, and within walking distance. It was close enough their passengers happily made their way to the diner during the stopovers. Having first-hand knowledge of the timetable made life easier for Merry, and it allowed her to plan ahead for the onslaught of guests she might have.

Still, it was hit and miss whether they visited the diner. A number of passengers went straight to *Candies Galore* and spent all their money there before embarking on the next leg of their journey. Since it had become somewhat famous, at least.

The next onslaught of passengers was due in around ten minutes, and Merry was taking a much deserved break while she waited for them to arrive. A large pot of thick beef and vegetable soup simmered on the stove, and there were four trays of hot bread rolls in her large oven. It was the most wholesome, and most requested meal for the short time they had available to eat between stops. Merry, was of course, prepared for other menu items should they be requested.

She took a deep breath and let it out slowly, then savored the hot coffee sitting in front of her. Soon this much needed break would be over, and she would again be run off her feet.

Merry had no sooner returned her empty mug to the kitchen, than she heard the front door open. She stood in the doorway to the kitchen watching passengers pushing and shoving each other trying to get in before everyone else, knowing their time was limited. What Merry really needed was help; someone who could help distribute meals when it was needed. If they knew their way around the kitchen, even better. She'd tried in vain, but so far had found no one suitable.

Well, mulling it over was not going to help, so she went to greet her newly arrived customers.

Nearly an hour later, and Merry felt ready to collapse. The stagecoach was at full capacity today. One poor woman had two young children with her, and was forced to hold them for the entire trip. Luckily, she didn't have much further to go.

"Would bribery help keep them in line?" she whispered to the mother, then told her about *Candies Galore*. The poor woman was ecstatic at the prospect.

There was a huge pile of dirty dishes waiting for her in the kitchen, but she was totally exhausted, and it was the last thing Merry felt like doing. She tried to talk herself out of it, but knew the task had to be done today, otherwise she would be behind before she even began work in the morning. The thought made her feel ill.

Every day it felt as though she was chasing her tail. She began the day preparing breakfast, then the moment the diner was cleared, cleaned up and began work on the luncheon meals. On the days she made stew, she began far earlier as it took much long to cook.

Merry staggered into the kitchen and poured herself a mug of coffee. She would take a few minutes to recover before tackling the dishes and cleaning down the tables. When she eyed the large pile of dishes, she groaned. The stack seemed almost insurmountable.

She really did need to find help. It wasn't like she couldn't afford to pay someone, especially on the days the stagecoach arrived in Dewberry. It was simply that she was unable to locate someone who had worked in a diner before, or even understood how a diner worked. The hospitality industry was not big in Dewberry, and therefore workers were not readily available. The thought was almost enough to make her cry. At least her mother had Merry to help her out, but Merry had no one.

Instead of dwelling on what she didn't have, Merry knew she should be counting her blessings for what she did have. She poured a coffee while she waited for the water to boil for the dishes. Then sat at one of the tables near the back and sipped her much needed coffee. The diner was closed now, so she wouldn't be disturbed. Thank goodness for small mercies.

She hadn't been seated even three minutes when she heard a noise. She really should have locked the door, but her energy was far too depleted to walk the short distance to the door to lock it. She glanced up. *Was someone here?* She couldn't see anyone.

There it was again. *It sounded like a groan?* She wasn't afraid, just curious, as she was certain everyone had left. If they were from the stagecoach crowd, they were in for bad news. The coach would have left by now. At least five minutes ago, perhaps longer.

Placing her mug on the table, Merry cautiously headed toward the front of the diner. Head on the table, mussed hair going this way and that, she couldn't tell if it was a man or woman. She glanced out the window; no one was about, so she prayed whoever was in her little diner was not violent. She wasn't sure she could protect herself.

Unless… she could run to the kitchen and grab a small pot. She could get more force behind a smaller pot than a larger one.

Yes, that's what she would do.

Before she could move, she heard the groan again. This time the head with the mussed up hair came up. "Where am…"

His eyes fluttered. The stranger could barely keep them open.

Her heart pounded. *Was she safe here alone with a strange man?* She hadn't had the chance to grab a pot yet, so would have to improvise should the necessity arise. She glanced about. All that was nearby was sugar bowl and the salt and pepper shakers. It became quite apparent she had little chance to defend herself should she need to.

"Who are you, and what are you doing in my diner?" She made certain her words were stern, and her voice authoritarian. As his head came further up, Merry recognized him. "Oh, you ate here earlier." Instead of being scared as she had been moments ago, she felt compassion toward him. "You've missed the stage."

His head shot up. "I can't have! I am due in Hamilton in two days." He groaned then, as though it was dire he get to his destination on time.

Before Merry could say anything more, he shoved his hand toward her. "Phillip Dalton," he said. "But everyone calls me Phil."

"Merry Jensen. I own this diner."

"Nice to meet you. I guess I'll have to get the stage tomorrow."

She grimaced. "I hate to be the one to break it to you, but the stagecoach only comes through Dewberry once a week." He stared at her and groaned. "We're small and out of the way. We're lucky to get the service at all." She shrugged.

"I suppose you are right. Well, I have no idea what I'll do now. That job was to be my fresh start." Phillip lay his head on the table again, as if in defeat. Merry couldn't help but feel sorry for him.

"Can you send them a telegraph and tell them you will be delayed?"

He lifted his head again. "I could, and will, but I doubt it will appease them. Perhaps you can tell me where I can get cheap accommodation until I can leave? I was counting on that job to keep me afloat."

Merry gave him directions to the saloon, and Phillip headed toward the door. "If you hear of any short term jobs, I'd appreciate it." And then he was gone, leaving a bewildered Merry in his wake.

The door to the diner opened, and it took a moment for Merry to realize the young man standing there was the one she'd spoken to earlier that day. Phillip had cleaned up, and was far better presented. He wore clean clothes, his hair was no longer a mess. He was more than presentable now.

"You look like a different person." He did, and she wanted him to know it.

"It's amazing what a bath and clean clothes can do. I was exhausted from days of traveling, and that didn't help either." He glanced about the empty diner, seemingly taking stock of the layout. "I don't suppose you heard of anyone looking for workers?"

Should she take the chance? It would only be for a week at most. Merry scanned him from head to toe. He scrubbed up pretty well, but the way he'd looked earlier, she wouldn't even consider taking him on. "No, but if you're interested..." She should have kept her mouth shut, but it was too late for that. She had no idea what his skill set even was.

"You're looking for someone? I'd be happy to take whatever work you can give me."

It was too late to turn back now, and she knew it. "I am always run off my feet, and haven't been able to find anyone local. I guess a week is better than nothing."

He stepped forward and took both her hands in his. "Thank you," he said, as he squeezed her hands in gratitude. "Anything you need done, I'm your man."

"I'm offering a dollar a day."

He considered that for a minute, then nodded. "Agreed. It's enough to pay for my lodgings, and if I'm frugal enough, should cover meals as well. Besides, it's only for a week, until I can get to Hamilton."

"I'll provide your meals as part of your wages. Does that sound all right to you?"

His eyes opened wide in amazement. "You don't have to do that. I'm happy to…"

"That's the deal, take it or leave it," she said, then turned and made her way to the kitchen. It was obvious Phillip was short on money, and the last thing she wanted was to see him starve. It wasn't as though he didn't want to work; he had a job waiting for him already, once he was able to get there.

Merry could hear him following behind her, and smiled. It would be wonderful having some help for a change, even if it was only short-term. She suddenly stopped and he ran into her back. His arms came up to steady her, and it felt nice. Her heart fluttered, but Merry knew she should think nothing of it. Phillip was only trying to stop her from falling.

"Sorry," he said as she turned to face him.

"Totally my fault. I suddenly realized I have no idea what skills you have, if any." She raised her eyebrows as she waited for an answer.

"Anything you need, I can do."

She ran her hands down her apron. "Anything?"

"Absolutely. Would you like a demonstration?"

She almost chuckled, but he was dead serious, so she held back her laughter. "Hmmm, well, if you can wipe down the tables, that would be great. They should be cleaned between each customer, of course, so if you can do that, as well as serve the food to the customers after I've made their meal, that would be very helpful. Oh, and wash dishes." The bane of her life was dirty dishes.

He stared at her for long moments before answering. "I can do that." He went to the sink and grabbed a wet kitchen cloth, then headed back to the diner. He appeared to be fighting a grin, but Merry couldn't figure out why. *What would make him treat this like a joke?* He was desperate, and she was helping him out.

She stirred the stew that was simmering on the stove, checked the roast lamb in the oven, then began to prepare biscuits. Lots of them. Most nights she went through dozens of biscuits, and sometimes still ran out. She was never able to predict how much of anything she made would be sold, but biscuits were the worst of all.

Merry added the flour and other ingredients to a large bowl, and combined the mixture. She then sprinkled flour on the countertop and began to knead it, then finally rolled it out. Phillip returned to the kitchen as she was adding them to the trays.

"You prepare well ahead," he said, as he returned the cloth to the sink and cleaned it. He watched her every move, and Merry found it unnerving. She wasn't used to being watched while she worked. "Would you like me to greet the customers as they arrive? It would save you quite a bit of time." She stared at him. She'd been doing that job for as long as she could remember, even when her mother was alive.

"If you think it's something you can do. Thank you."

"I'm certain I can." There was that smirk again, only this time he hadn't managed to hide it as well as he did earlier. She wasn't sure what that was about.

"Bottom draw in the center cupboard, you should find some aprons."

He openly chuckled this time. "Not frilly ones like the one you're wearing I hope," he said, then began to rummage through the drawer. There weren't a lot there, but Merry was certain there would be some plain aprons. Mother preferred those over the fancy type, but they were only the sort that tied around your waist. Merry had always had a preference for full aprons that protected her clothes. Far too feminine for a man, especially a man like Phillip.

Merry gasped. She had no idea where that thought had come from, and went back to stirring the stew, trying to distract herself. When she turned around again, the apron was around his waist, and looked as though it was meant to be there. It was like he'd done it a thousand times before.

"What do you think? Am I presentable?" He grinned.

She couldn't stop herself from staring. "Perfect," she said, right before licking her lips. Her heart fluttered, and she had no idea why. This man, this absolute stranger was making her feel things she'd never felt before. It was as though he mattered, which was the oddest thing. They'd known each other less than a day.

The door to the diner opened, and Phillip rushed out to greet the first customers of the evening. Merry pulled the roast from the oven and checked it. Total perfection. The desserts were cooked earlier in the day, and ready to go. She even had those dished up for when they were ordered. She ran a structured kitchen. Having Phillip here to help would surely prove her to be more organized than before.

He was soon back in the kitchen with the first order of the evening. Table of four, and the order was for four roasts. The dinner plates were on the side of the countertop waiting to be filled. As she carved, he filled four tumblers with water and took them out to the table. Already he had earned today's dollar, and the night had barely begun.

As the night drew on, Merry was far more grateful for the additional help than she thought she would be. It had been an exceptionally busy night, and apart from the fact that Christmas was drawing nearer, she had no idea why. Families were out and about more this time of year, doing their Christmas shopping. More recently, one of the drawcards to Dewberry Lane had been *Candies Galore* and their now famous candies. She wasn't complaining.

Instead of running backwards and forwards between the front of house and the kitchen, Merry had spent a leisurely evening dishing out meals. The biscuits had come close to running out, and she'd made yet another batch. As she placed them in the oven, Phillip entered the kitchen. "Those biscuits of yours are incredibly popular. What do you put in them?"

"Nothing special. But I don't charge for them." She waited for his admonishment. It was a bad business move and she knew it. She'd previously been told it was costing her money – some customers filled up on the free biscuits and ordered little else.

Phillip stood there for what seemed like forever, without speaking, his face taut. Then it softened as he began to speak. "You're being taken advantage of," he said gently. "An easy way to stop it, is to supply the first plate free, then charge after that."

She gaped at him. He was right – it was the perfect solution. *Why hadn't she thought of it herself?* "You've worked in a diner before, haven't you,

Phillip?" Merry was kicking herself. Now that she had the time to breathe, it was clear he had.

"Phil," he said. "It's that obvious?" He chuckled then. The front door opened again, and he made his retreat to greet the latest customers.

She could get used to hearing his voice each day, but had to resign herself to the fact he was only here until the stagecoach arrived next week.

Merry went back to plating the orders, and contemplated doing this alone again.

Chapter Two

Phil washed while Merry dried. To an outsider, the pile of dishes would seem insurmountable, but he'd seen it all before. And handled it all by himself when necessary. *Ma's Kitchen* was tiny compared to his last position, but he liked it here. It was a pity Joe's Eatery had burned down, but when someone is determined to destroy a business, they'll do whatever it takes.

Not that he'd had much chance to see a lot of the town, but what he'd seen of Dewberry so far appealed to him. *Bert's Eating House* in Hamilton, where he was due to start working, promised to be far bigger. And much busier. He liked the pace of the diner here. There wasn't the same level of stress as the last place, but Bert's was sure to be near frantic at times.

He sighed. Well, a week here would be like a holiday he guessed. With Christmas not far away, it was sure to get busier. "You need to rearrange your cupboards," he said without thinking. "A tiny thing like you must have difficulties reaching those plates."

He glanced down at her. Merry was scowling, then suddenly a smile filled her face. "You're right. I've climbed those steps to pull them down for so long, it's become habit. My mother was taller than me, and it was easier for her."

He opened the waist-height cupboards to check where the plates could be stored and found huge piles of kitchen towels on a lower shelf. "There's an empty drawer over there," he said, pointing. "That would free up this lower cupboard for your crockery."

He'd worried she'd be annoyed, but instead, Merry looked pleased. He would do as much as he could to help before he left. It was the least he could do. She'd got him out of a difficult situation, and he was beyond grateful to her.

"You certainly know what you're doing in a kitchen."

If only she knew. He had thought of telling her, but for the week he would be here, it wasn't worth the effort. Besides, she'd get used to it, and where would that leave her? This time next week he would start his new job, and Merry would be alone again.

He shook himself mentally. This would not do. What happened to the owner of this diner was not his problem or his business. He would advise where he saw changes could be made to make her life easier, but that was it.

His problem had always been getting himself too entrenched. Taking on the worries of the business, and taking far too much on his shoulders. But this was different. Merry was a decent person, unlike some of his former employers. The state he was in when he arrived – most people would have thrown him out of their establishment and banished them for life. Not Merry. She'd taken pity on him, and ensured he had a job and enough food in his belly.

Speaking of food…his stomach rumbled. Merry laughed, and the sound hit him like a punch to the gut. "I guess it is time we ate. There is left over roast and stew, and not much else. Oh, and biscuits." She grinned at mention of biscuits, and his heart flipflopped.

Phillip didn't understand these feelings that hit him so hard. He had to keep reminding himself he was only there for a week. Otherwise he would have a full belly and a place to stay, but his heart might not be intact by the time he left. He inwardly groaned. That was the last thing he needed.

They sat opposite each other in the diner. Hot food piled high on his plate, Phil was grateful for this delicious meal. It was far better than anything he'd seen at the saloon. He wouldn't even call it food, more like muck. No wonder *Ma's Diner* was doing so well. Merry was a great cook, and that alone would draw the customers in. Apart from the fact it was the only other eating establishment in this part of town. Not that he'd explored the town much, the farthest he'd got was to the telegraph office to let Bert's know he wouldn't make it on time.

He had to hope they wouldn't hold it against him. He was exhausted from the long trip, so it was no wonder he'd fallen asleep. He had no one to blame but himself. At least he had his luggage – when he'd missed the deadline, they'd removed his belongings and left them in the office. Thank goodness for small mercies, as his mother always said. He now fully understand the meaning of her mantra.

After they'd eaten and readied the diner for service the next day, Phil offered to walk Merry home. Not only was it snowing, albeit lightly, but it was pitch black apart from the moonlight. She'd balked of course, but he'd insisted. He would not have her on his conscious. Not that he expected something to happen to her, but you never knew who might be around and what they might do. Any true gentleman would do the same.

As it happened, he was pleased he'd insisted on accompanying her. A group of about ten young men loitered in their path. He watched as they ogled her, and felt far better having walked her home. He could only imagine how intimidated Merry would have felt having to pass them alone at night. She lived within walking distance of the diner, but it was on the edge of town, and quite a distance for her to walk alone in the dark.

It bothered Phil, and he would make certain to walk her home each night, but knew once he left she'd be on her own again.

"Here we are," she said brightly. "I would have been fine, but thank you. I do appreciate it."

He stared down into her moonlit face. She was a beautiful woman, he knew that already. But with the moonlight dancing across her face, she was far more lovely than he'd even realized. She glanced up at him, and stared. When she licked her lips, he was tempted to lean in and kiss her.

But he had no right, and most importantly, Merry would be infuriated. He knew she would. He wasn't sure what compelled him to have such feelings, but Phil knew he had to fight them. They would be working together for the next several days, and he didn't want to jeopardize their working relationship. If he lost this job due to his stupidity, he had no idea what he would do. Not only would he have to find money for his accommodation, he would also have to pay for food. Disgusting food at that, since he'd have to buy it from the saloon.

Phil sighed as he shook himself mentally. He would keep his distance, but how he would do that while he worked at the diner, he had no idea.

"I prefer to get you home safely. I'm not sure about those young men. Do you know them?"

She was thoughtful for a moment. "I have seen them around, but I don't know them personally."

He was right to worry, and he would ensure he got her home safely each night. But what would happen beyond the week? It was a pity he couldn't stay on, but he'd already accepted a position elsewhere, and Merry hadn't indicated he'd be welcome to work for her permanently. *Was it even something he would accept should she make that offer?* Especially when he knew he was already attracted to the pretty diner owner.

Phil was up early and waited outside the diner for his employer. It might only be temporary, but Merry was still his employer and he wanted to please her.

He was earlier than required, but she had shown him kindness, and he intended to return the favor. The diner was always busy for breakfast she'd told him, and he wanted to help where possible. It was obvious from yesterday's service, this little diner was busy all the time. How she'd managed alone, he had no idea, but while it was possible, he would give her as much help as he possibly could.

She paid well, plus she was supplying his meals as well. Phil couldn't be more pleased about the arrangement. He was going to pay her back in kind, no matter her protests.

He turned as he saw movement out the corner of his eye. He could have picked her up from home, but didn't want it to seem…weird or creepy. He trusted those young men only hung about late at night, otherwise he would have collected her for sure.

"Good morning," she said before he had a chance to open his mouth. "You're early." She glanced at him quizzically. He was far earlier than the time they'd agreed upon, but he was used to getting up this early, and was eager to help her.

He shrugged. "I'm used to the early hours." She smiled then, and a shiver ran down his spine. *When did a woman's smile make him react this way?* To be truthful, he'd never reacted to anyone like this. It was completely new to him. "What's on the agenda today?"

Her eyes opened wide in question. "The same as every other day. I'll prepare breakfast, and then the diner will fill. I'll wash the dishes, and then prepare lunch. Wash dishes, prepare supper, wash dishes again. And on it goes."

She didn't look exactly happy about the prospect, and Phil guessed the business was wearing her down. If only he could stay and help her out, even if only for a few weeks. But he knew that was impossible. What he proposed was impractical, not to mention impossible, no matter which way he looked at it.

"At least you have me to help you out for a while."

She glanced up into his face. "There's that." She closed her eyes momentarily as if thinking about the prospect. "It would be wonderful if it was for longer. Yesterday was the easiest day I've had for an incredibly long time. It's certainly been difficult."

He wasn't sure what to say, so said nothing. Staying was not an option as he'd already accepted another position in another town. Merry was aware of that, and seemed mindful of that fact.

"I know you can't stay," Merry said as she unlocked the door to *Ma's Diner*. "It would be nice, but we both know it's not an option." She turned to him then and smiled tentatively. "More's the pity."

His heart thudded. He truly wished it was possible. He dearly wanted to stay, yearned to stay, but *Bert's Eating House* would not be thrilled at the prospect.

They'd sought him out after the fire at Joe's. If the choice had been there, Phil would have stayed at Joe's Diner. But the owner had decided to collect the insurance money and move on. Given someone was out to get him and close his business down, for a reason unknown to anyone including the police, it seemed the right decision to make.

"I wish I could stay. Dewberry seems a nice place to settle down." And it did. But if he stayed on, what were his prospects? Go into competition with Merry? An outsider competing against a local? That wouldn't work, and he knew it. Or maybe she would want him to work with her.

Phil shook himself mentally. The honest truth was, no matter how much he debated it in his head, the option simply wasn't available. He had an agreement to work at Bert's, and that was that.

Merry locked the door behind them. It was far too early for customers to be accepted, and she told him she had no intention of allowing them in before opening time. She hurried to the kitchen and picked up some logs to add to the fire. "Here, let me," Phil said, taking the logs from her hands. Their fingers brushed and she glanced up at him. Color flooded her cheeks, and he wondered had a thrill traveled up her arms as it had for him.

He opened the door to the stove and shook up the embers, then added some small twigs and logs, along with some old newspapers. When he was satisfied with the level of the fire, he added some larger logs. A filled kettle already sat on the stove; he'd filled it last night before they left. With the fire burning strongly, it shouldn't be long before it was boiling, and he could make coffee. Black and strong – it's what they both needed at this time of the day. The sun was barely over the horizon, and what an amazing image it made.

He stood at the kitchen window watching it, before he came back to the present.

"Beautiful, isn't it?"

Merry's voice rolled through him like the warmth of the sun. He couldn't recall a time he'd been so happy. Perhaps it was knowing he wouldn't be caught up in the hustle and bustle of a busy diner like Joe's or Bert's, or maybe it was merely being with Merry.

He had a sneaky suspicion it was the latter, but he pushed that thought to the back of his mind. He needed to concentrate on surviving the next week before moving on to Hamilton.

He pulled two mugs from the cupboard, and waited for the kettle to boil. "What can I do to help?" She was busy preparing the frypans for the breakfast service.

"I'm fine." She glanced across at him. Phil knew his expression would be one of disbelief. "Honestly? You're going to give me *that* look?" She laughed then, and Phil reveled in the sound. She had the most amazing laugh, and it made her entire face light up.

"What's on the menu?"

"I usually make bacon, sausages, and eggs. Tomatoes too when they're in season."

"And..."

"And nothing. That's breakfast." She suddenly looked guilty. But she had no need to feel that way – she worked alone and couldn't manage additional choices.

He sighed. "Will you trust me to add to your breakfast menu today?" He wasn't sure if this was the right thing to do, but wanted to do it anyway. "I promise you will be able to handle it yourself once I'm gone."

She studied him. He wasn't sure if she didn't trust him, or was mulling over the part about when he was gone. Phil didn't blame her.

"What do you have in mind?"

Perhaps she was open to ideas after all. "Scrambled eggs with bacon and toast for one option. Pancakes and maple syrup for another."

She didn't say a word, and he was certain she would refuse the request. Suddenly she began rifling through the pantry. "I don't have any maple syrup. The mercantile should carry it though." She smiled then, and his heart fluttered. "They'll be open shortly, so by the time you've done your preparation, it will be time to go there."

Phil waited for the inevitable questions, but they never came. Wasn't she even in the slightest curious about his ability to make these menu items? If their positions were reversed, he was certain he'd want to know. Instead of giving her the opportunity, he began to mix the ingredients for each of his chosen breakfast dishes. There was no way to tell how many customers would order his items, but he figured being new on the menu, they would likely be popular.

Before he knew it, it was time to visit the mercantile.

Phil carried two plates of pancakes out to table five. Merry followed behind. He couldn't believe how nervous he felt – as though it was his first time making pancakes. It wasn't – far from it. But it was his first time making them for his current employer.

Placing the plates in front of each person seated at the table, he tried not to let his nerves show, though his hands were visibly shaking. *What was that about?* He placed a jug of maple syrup on the table between the customers, then stood back. "Enjoy," he said, turning to leave. Merry blocked his path.

The first customer took a bite of the now syrup-covered pancakes. "Mmmm, this is delicious," he said.

The second customer reiterated that opinion.

Phil let go of the breath he'd been holding, and Merry winked at him, then they both returned to the kitchen. "Your pancakes are a hit already," she told him, clearly elated at the result.

The morning went quickly, with pancakes being the most requested breakfast item of the day. They were so popular he needed to make two more batches of his light-as-a-feather pancakes. The diner was busier than it had been for quite some time according to Merry. Word must have spread like wildfire.

She glanced around the kitchen as the door to the diner opened once more. "Brace yourself," she said under her breath as she hurried out to the diner. *A difficult customer?* He was about to find out.

"Good morning, Mrs. Grayson," Merry said cheerfully. "I'd like you to meet Phillip Dalton. He's helping out for a few days."

"Phil," he said, offering his hand to the newcomer, but she only stared at it.

"Welcome Mr. Dalton." She studied him, and Phil felt like an ant under a microscope. He wondered if she was like this with everyone. "I heard you are offering pancakes for breakfast today." She raised her eyebrows and studied Phil again. "Your doing, I suppose." It was a statement, not a question, so he didn't bother answering. He had enough trouble holding back a grin as it was.

"Would you like some, Mrs. Grayson?" Merry stepped closer to the elderly woman.

"Yes, thank you, my dear. I would like that."

Luckily there was still plenty of batter left. This customer looked like she meant business. *Was she some sort of food critic?* She certainly came across that way. He headed toward the kitchen and began work. It wasn't long before he had the pancakes plated, and a jug of maple syrup prepared and on the tray. Merry went ahead of him and poured Mrs. Grayson a strong black coffee. When she'd finished, he placed the pancakes in front of the elderly woman, and the jug of syrup in the middle of the table.

They both watched in anticipation as she took a mouthful. Suddenly, she let out a screech startling them both. "Oh my goodness," she continued when she'd calmed down. Phil's heart thudded. She hated them, and now the woman would give Merry's store a bad review. "These are the absolute best pancakes I have *ever* eaten."

Phil sighed with relief. "Thank you, Ma'am," he said and began to back away.

"No, wait," she said urgently. "What other delicacies will you be creating?"

"Scrambled eggs and bacon, Ma'am."

She turned to Merry. "I like him – his food anyway. You hang onto him, young lady."

Merry's face dropped. "Phil is only here for a week – until the stage comes through again."

"Then find a way to keep him here." She waved Merry away, effectively dismissing her, and Phil turned to leave as well. "You, Mr. Dalton, sit down." This was a woman used to getting her own way, and he complied. "Tell me, does Miss Jensen know you're a chef and not merely a server?"

"How…?" He was flummoxed. He'd not told a soul in Dewberry.

"I'm a woman of means; I've traveled far and wide. This is not the food of an amateur." She filled her mouth again. "These pancakes melt in your mouth." She glanced down at her plate and stared for long moments, setting him on edge. "You can't leave Dewberry. It would be absolutely criminal." After uttering those words, she waved him away, and continued to eat.

What Merry would say about these revelations, he had no idea.

Chapter Three

"I need to tell you something." He had to confess to his temporary employer, or Mrs. Grayson would surely do it. Not that he knew the woman, but he got the impression she wasn't one to mess with. One thing was for sure, she was used to getting her own way.

Merry turned to face him. As much as they tried, it was difficult to keep on top of the dishes throughout the meal service. He mentally shook his head trying to fathom how Merry had managed the diner alone all this time. Not for a lack of trying – she'd told him she couldn't get anyone local to work for her. It wasn't the money, it was the hard and constant work involved. Phil was used to it, and didn't even notice it now.

He'd left school and gone straight into the food business. It helped that his uncle was a chef and trained him from a young age. *That way I can teach you the way I want you to learn*, he'd said. And it had worked. He'd had several jobs after Uncle George had died suddenly. Phil would have bought the business had it been possible, but it was snatched away before he could even apply for a loan.

Then again, he wouldn't have ended up in Dewberry, never would have met Merry, or had the privilege to learn about this quaint little diner.

Merry stopped what she was doing and waited. He took a deep breath and mentally counted to ten. This would be amongst one of the hardest things he'd had to do. Crazy when they barely knew each other. He opened his mouth, but the words didn't come.

She frowned. "Is it that bad?" She studied him then. "You're leaving already?"

His heart thudded. *Did she really think he'd abandon her?* Besides, he needed this job, and without it, wouldn't survive until the stagecoach arrived. "No, nothing like that," he said far quicker than he'd anticipated. "It's just, well, Mrs. Grayson guessed, and I thought I'd best tell you…"

He stopped then. She'd gone pale, and Phil worried she might faint. "Do you want to sit down?"

"Do I need to?" She leaned against the nearest cupboard for support. He really needed to just blurt it out.

"I have been working in diners and restaurants since I left school." She raised her eyebrows then, suddenly more interested than before. "I'm not a server, although as you've seen, I can clearly do that job."

She leaned a little closer than before. "So you're a…?"

His breath whooshed, and he hurried the words. "I'm a trained chef. I've worked as Head Chef for several of the biggest restaurants across several states." He let that sink in and was about to continue when she stumbled. Phil hurried toward her and held her around the waist. It felt good. He brushed the thought away, then sat her down and she stared up at him.

"And I'm paying you a dollar a day." Her eyes were wide in disbelief. "Why didn't you tell me?"

"Because you don't need a chef, and I'm only here for a matter of days." She nodded, but she didn't look convinced. "If it hadn't been for Mrs. Grayson, I probably wouldn't have told you at all."

"Mrs. Grayson?"

He smiled tentatively then. "She guessed. Said she's a *woman of means* and knew quality food." At the time he was floored, but now saw it as a compliment of the highest order. However, that didn't get him out of the predicament he found himself in right now. He waited for Merry to send him packing, and held his breath, a habit he had when stressed or worried.

"I don't know what to say." Her voice was quiet, only just above a whisper. Suddenly a slow smile crossed her face. She tapped a finger on her chin, then grinned. "Should we make the most of it while you're still here? Can I impose?"

Impose? He would be delighted. Phil enjoyed cooking, and it was killing him to have to serve tables and watch Merry struggle alone in the kitchen. Especially during the busy times. "It's no imposition; I would love to help out."

Between service, they worked on a new temporary menu. One that Phil would fulfill until he had to leave. This menu would be special, and he chose a number of his most favorite dishes. Many that rarely saw the light of day. They were a little more expensive than Merry's average price range, but they figured the customers wouldn't mind paying a little more for such delicacies.

On the menu were items such as Pot-au-feu, or French beef stew as it was commonly known. He also included his own version of Tourte au poule, or Chicken Pot Pie, not to mention his famous roast lamb. Phil would ensure there were a number of more exotic desserts to entice the customers too. He was near salivating at the thought of all the delicious meals he would create over the coming days.

Each day would be something different, to keep the customers coming back. His only regret was that he would be gone far too soon. Merry was a wonderful person, and as an employer, she was amongst the best he'd had.

He shook himself mentally. He had to stop thinking about Dewberry – he had another job arranged, and he had to fulfill his promise there. As much as he was becoming accustomed to this wonderful little town, he had to brush those thoughts aside and think of the future. *Bert's Eating House* was famous, at least in Montana. It wasn't his first choice, but the only place with vacancies at the time.

But his mind should be on creating menus and meals, and not on anything else. *Wasn't that how he'd come as far as he had?* By ensuring the current job received his undivided attention? And he would ensure it stayed that way.

Phil reached for the paper Merry had given him, and wrote out the next menus – for the kitchen at least. Because they wouldn't be permanent menus, he decided a blackboard menu would be best for the diner. Each day it could be easily updated, depending on what ingredients they were able to source. He always purchased fresh ingredients on a daily basis from the local market, so would have to consult with Merry about that possibility. He was really looking forward to this new venture with her.

And then it hit him. This was a short-term prospect, and in only a matter of days, he would be gone from Dewberry. Possibly forever. His head pounded. *Was that really what he wanted?* No matter, the choice was out of his hands. He had made arrangements for another position, and he had an obligation to fulfill.

He stared sadly down at the menus he had produced for the coming days. It had been exciting while it lasted, and he would do his best. He owed that much to Merry.

"We're going to run out of lard." Phil glanced up at Merry as he made yet another batch of puff pastry. His chicken pot pie was far more popular than either of them had envisaged. With mashed potatoes and beans on the side, it was a complete meal. Even without the vegetables it was a complete meal, and that's how they would serve it for lunch. At a reduced price, he didn't think the customers would be upset.

"If you're okay, I'll quickly run to the mercantile."

It would be a juggle on his own, but he would manage. The last thing they needed were angry patrons when they couldn't get the meal they wanted.

The chicken filling was ready and cooling, and all that was left to do was add the pastry and place the individual pies in the oven. This batch would be cooked by the time Merry returned, and then he could start on the next batch of pastry.

Phil stood back and eyed his handiwork. It felt good to be cooking again. He hadn't had this much fun for ages. He hadn't worked since Joe's burned down over a month ago, which was why he'd become so desperate. But he also hadn't cooked, and doing this now had filled a craving from deep inside him.

He had chosen Vanilla Blancmange for the dessert of the day, and had made it almost immediately after breakfast. It needed plenty of time to cool and set, and now it was ready for eating. After he'd cleaned up here, he would add the already prepared sugared cranberries as decoration for the Blancmange and finish it off with clotted cream.

It was a meal fit for a queen. It made him feel good to be offering such a delicious meal to the people of Dewberry, many of whom had no doubt never experienced such opulence.

Phil went out to the diner. It had been a while since Merry had left, and he hadn't checked on the customers. It was past time he did.

"The food is delicious," one woman said.

"It's absolutely gourmet," her companion added. He was well dressed, and Phil was certain he was well traveled. "I'll be returning again," he said. Phil didn't tell him that beyond a week, he wouldn't be here.

As he made his way through the little diner, the compliments continued. Never had his cooking been so highly praised. The people of Dewberry were rather sheltered with their dining experiences, so he took their compliments lightly. If they dined in Helena, for example, they would be sure to find cuisine equally as good.

Deep down, he knew that was untrue. He was well known in many circles as *the chef* if you wanted your restaurant or diner to thrive. Right now that was being said of *Ma's Diner*. He glanced around the room. The smiles on the guests' faces said it all. Right here and right now, he felt far more welcome than he'd felt for a very long time.

He felt at home here.

What if he was able to stay? What would happen then? Merry had indicated he'd be welcome to stay longer. But as it always did, it came back to the fact he had already accepted another job and had to move on.

Merry

The door to the diner suddenly flew open, and Merry, breathless as she was, came bowling through. "I got it," she said, holding up a brown paper bag. She then hurried into the kitchen.

Phil chatted briefly with some of the patrons, then made his way there as well. His steps were unhurried; there were no urgent chores to do right this moment. He would shortly take the remaining pies out of the oven, then would begin work on a new batch of pastry.

Phil smiled. He was right where he wanted to be. If only there was a way to be able to stay.

With the lunch service over, it was time to begin preparing for supper. Having the same featured dish each day made it far easier to plan ahead. Today, supper was the same, but included vegetables. Tomorrow and every day after that, things would be different – there would be time to plan ahead and ensure there was a better variety throughout the day. Not that customers were complaining, far from it, but Phil did like to mix things up, not just for the guests, but also for himself.

"Coffee?" Merry didn't wait for him to answer, but placed a mug of strong black coffee in front of him. Phil was resting at one of the dining tables, a habit he'd begun many years ago. Being on his feet all day long, and not taking a break was not productive. Nor was it good for his health.

She sat opposite, and lifted her own coffee to her lips. "Today has been wonderful. The customers were all very impressed. I just wish I'd had time to watch what you did. I can't believe you had these skills, and I was oblivious." She stared down into the mug of steaming liquid. "I wish you could stay," she said quietly.

Phil did too. Who knew stopping in this tiny town would renew his love of cooking? Not that he hated it. But it had almost become a chore. As much as he loved his last job, there wasn't the freedom to create whatever he wanted. Here, he had that freedom. Merry had allowed him to make whatever his heart craved, and that's when he was happiest and at his most creative. It filled his heart with joy.

Merry filled his heart with joy too.

He reached across the table, and covered her hand with his own. "I can't stay, we both know that." He stared into her eyes as a shot of electricity went down his spine, then took a sip of coffee trying to deny what had happened. Phil quickly pulled his hand away. Her eyes pierced his. It made him wonder if she'd felt it too.

"What if you could, would you?"

She was playing games with him now. The choice was not his to make. "If I could, I would certainly stay here in Dewberry. I'd stay working here too, if you'd have me."

"Without hesitation." Now it was her turn to cover his hand. Hers was tiny in comparison to his, and it made him smile. It made him think about how small she was, and how vulnerable she would be should something happen when she was here alone. He remembered when he walked her home, with those young men loitering across the street where she walked. Would they have been so compliant if she'd been alone? Phil didn't think so. It bothered him far more than he knew it should.

The conversation was getting them nowhere, and he didn't want Merry to think there was any chance he could stay. "I would change things if I could, but I'm due at Bert's next week. We both knew this was only temporary." He stood then, taking the last long draw on his coffee, then hurried toward the kitchen, then turned back. "I've decided to make a selection of cupcakes for tonight. Do you have time to help? I'll even give you my secret recipe."

He winked and watched as her cheeks bloomed into a pretty pink. Then headed quickly toward the kitchen before his heart decided to rule his head.

Chapter Four

With the diner full to overflowing for each meal service, Merry was now taking bookings. It was a first for the diner, but word had got around that Phillip Dalton, renowned chef, was in town. That such a person should be at *Ma's Kitchen* was something the town's people had no intention of ignoring. Merry was not going to pass up the opportunity, but was not looking forward to the time when Phil left and she was alone in the diner once more.

She'd watched over his shoulder as he'd made the cupcakes yesterday. Today he was making lemon cakes. Merry felt privileged to have a glimpse into his hallowed world of cooking. As she stood close to Phil, she felt comforted by his warmth, and it filled her entire being just being near to him. He took a step backwards and crashed into her. Despite their collision, and a tingle ran down her spine.

"Sorry," she said quietly, then stepped back out of his way.

"I'm looking for a grater," he said, then began to rifle through the cupboards.

Merry quickly found it and handed it over. Phil then grated the lemon rind and sprinkled it into the bowl. It was magical watching him work; he was a genius in the kitchen, and she'd never seen anything like it.

She knew she should walk away and find something else to do, but Merry was mesmerized by this gentle giant. How she ever thought he was a vagrant when she first found him, she would never know. Although he was rather disheveled, and he did carry a bit of an odor – from the constant travel he'd said. A bath and change of clothes, and he was a new man.

"Where did you come from?" She blurted the words out without thinking, and he turned to stare at her.

"Excuse me?" He looked rather confused.

"When you arrived in Dewberry, you said you'd traveled a long way. Where did you come from?"

He turned back to the cake he was making. "Cheyenne. I'd been traveling far longer than I'd envisaged. At least part of the trip was by train. Stagecoach is not fun when you're on it for days on end."

Phil was right. She'd taken short trips, and that was enough for her. Merry had become quite ill on her last stagecoach journey, and she'd vowed never to do it again.

He glanced at her, then went back to his baking again. He was so talented, and Merry fervently wished he could stay. She had to stop herself from going there, because it was a desire neither of them could achieve, and she knew it.

She greased the baking pans and placed them on the countertop. If memory served her well, these flat pans hadn't been used since before her mother died. Baking was not Merry's forte, nor did she enjoy it. She didn't mind cooking meals and desserts, and that's what she stuck to. No wonder her customers reveled in Phil's baking.

"I'm a terrible person." She said the words out loud, but hadn't meant to.

Phil stopped in his tracks. "Why would you say that? You seem perfectly wonderful to me." He flashed her a cheeky grin, and her entire body shivered. *How could such simple words make her feel this way?*

"Watching you has reminded me how much the Dewberry customers always loved Ma's baking. I don't like it much, and never do it."

"Well now you've got me." Only she didn't, and his smile quickly turned to a frown. "I didn't mean… Sorry," he said, and reached out a hand to her. Every time they touched, she yearned for more. Getting close to Phil was a bad idea. A very bad idea. He would be leaving soon, and her heart would feel empty again. She enjoyed their time together, but since it wouldn't last, couldn't last, she had to keep her distance.

Merry vowed to do just that.

She stood back and watched as he filled the baking tins, then placed them in the oven. He quickly cleaned up, and then began to wash the dishes. "That's my job. You baked, I get the fun job." She pulled a face and he laughed. Merry loved listening to his laugh. Heck, she liked listening to him, period. And looking at him and standing near him. She liked everything about him. But from this moment on, she would keep as far away from him as she could, and wouldn't even stay in the same room as Phil.

She wondered how long she could keep up the pretense.

The lemon cakes turned out beautifully. Not that there was ever any doubt. As she continued to clean up the kitchen, Phil prepared the icing. They would make a wonderful addition to the dessert menu tonight, and her customers would revel in it. She glanced over her shoulder and studied him as he decorated each cake. What he did seemed effortless, but Merry knew it was a matter of practice. He'd done it for so long, it was child's play. At least she assumed it was. When he'd finished he called her over. "I'm going to need a display tray or plate. Something. Do you have a dessert platter?"

She stared at the lemon cakes spread over the countertop. They looked delicious, and so very appealing. She could already imagine the diners drooling over these delicacies and knew they would sell out.

Phil suddenly dipped his finger into the leftover icing. "Come closer," he instructed, and she did. Without warning, he placed his icing covered finger in her mouth. Her tastebuds reacted to the flavors bursting there, and she wanted more.

"The icing is exploding with flavor," she said quietly. Afraid if she said too much aloud, her true feelings might come to the surface, she suddenly stopped talking. Her biggest fear wasn't the flavor, nor was it how she would continue where Phil began. Her greatest fear was the way she was beginning to feel about this man.

They'd spent several days together now, and already Merry worried how she would cope without him. But it was more. Much more, and she knew it.

Phil had already begun to get under her skin. He had been the perfect partner for her and *Ma's Diner*, and deep down she'd known it almost from the start. Even before she'd discovered he was a famous chef, she sensed there was something special about him. Not only on a professional level.

The trouble was Phil would be leaving in a matter of days, and there was nothing either of them could do about it. It was good having him here, but she had to get used to not having him around again. The thought had her swallowing back her emotions. Merry wasn't sure she wanted to get used to it.

He stared down into her face. "It's good, right?"

She knew he was asking about the icing, but for Merry, it was far more. It was the culmination of the icing, and Phil's nearness. Having his skin so close to hers set off her nerve endings, and sent warmth shooting through her body. He abruptly pulled his finger away, as though he now realized what an intimate act it was.

"It was my uncle's secret recipe." he said quietly, staring down into her face. "Sorry," he finally said, as though he only now realized the implications of what he'd done.

She tried to pull her eyes away, but Merry felt mesmerized by his presence, and gazed back at him. Before she could stop herself, she licked her lips. His hands came up and cupped her face, and his head came slowly down. Her heart pounded, but she didn't pull away. Soon his lips were covering hers, but Merry didn't complain, and she didn't refuse. She closed her eyes and reveled in the here and now.

The kiss was brief, as though he wasn't sure if it was acceptable, and Merry leaned against him. She sighed, not sure whether it was because the kiss had finished or because she wanted it to continue.

What she did know was that Phil would be leaving soon, and this behavior was inappropriate when there was no possibility of a relationship between the two of them.

After all, the stagecoach would be here in only a matter of days, and that would be the last she would ever see of Phillip Dalton, chef extraordinaire.

What did he just do? Phil silently admonished and mentally slapped himself. The pull toward Merry had been tremendous, and he couldn't help himself. But that was no excuse. He should have been more restrained, kept his distance. After all, that's what he'd promised himself he would do. It wouldn't be long, and he would be gone from here, so starting something was not appropriate, in any circumstances.

He'd vowed to help Merry until he left, but that didn't include helping himself to her lips, and wrapping her in his arms. *What was he thinking?* The last thing he wanted was to compromise her reputation. They only got away with being alone because they were working together, otherwise it wouldn't have been allowed at all.

His heart was still pounding from the moment their lips met, and he knew there was more to this than an employer and employee situation. He was falling in love with her. On the other hand, their close proximity on a daily basis could be fooling him into thinking that was the case.

That said, he'd worked with women before and not felt this way. He watched as she scurried out of the kitchen. She hadn't said no, and he would never force a woman, not to kiss him, or anything else. True gentlemen didn't behave in that manner. Phil suddenly felt hot, and he knew it was not the cooking or the oven causing the soar in temperature. It was the way he'd held Merry. And kissed her. He picked up the recipe sheets he'd written and left on the countertop, fanning his face with them.

Now that he'd gotten that out of his system, perhaps they could move forward and simply work together.

He nodded. Yes, that's how it would be. They could return to normal and have a regular working relationship. Only Phil knew that was the farthest thing from the truth.

The supper service was a roaring success, and Phil's Lemon Cakes sold out in record time. Whatever he chose for tomorrow's dessert, he needed to produce more. Far more. To have patrons leaving feeling they'd missed out was the ultimate compliment to the chef, but the worst case scenario for the customers.

He needed to do better. The trouble was every day they had more and more customers. That would die down to a steady flow, it usually did, but it was already at a point where Merry needed additional staff. Trained waiting staff, but none were available.

Phil might be leaving soon, but he had no intention of leaving a potential mess behind for Merry to clean up. Right now he wanted to stomp his foot and have a tantrum. Only he was far too old for that. What he needed to do was find a way to stay here. He really enjoyed being side by side with Merry. She was a terrific cook, and he enjoyed working with her.

She wasn't a trained chef like he was, but that didn't matter. She was far better than any of the sous chefs he'd worked with over the years, probably due to her mother, who he'd heard was an amazing cook.

If he was honest with himself, Phil would know that wasn't the reason he wanted to stay. Only he refused to be honest, and didn't want to admit he was falling in love with the petite young woman who owned

Ma's Diner. He knew the diner could be built up into something very unique if he were to stay. But it wouldn't be as special as the relationship he knew he and Merry could build.

As he created an omelet for himself and Merry for their supper, since there was little left over now, these thoughts all ran through his head. He felt tortured by the fact he had to leave this quaint little town he'd grown to love, even in this short period of time.

"Is there a way…" Merry's voice cut into his thoughts, but she stopped as suddenly as she began. When he glanced across at her, she was shaking her head.

"Is there a way…?" He studied her. She seemed far more relaxed than she was when they first met. He hoped that was because of him. Because of what he'd done here.

"Forget it. It will never happen, so I'm not even going to ask." She suddenly turned and walked away. She had him curious, but Phil would quiz her further while they ate. He expertly flipped their omelet, then plated it up ready for eating.

He carried the two plates out to the diner and sat opposite Merry. She'd already placed a mug of coffee for each of them, and the table was set as though they were guests of the diner. It was a nice touch.

He reached for her hands and said a quick blessing. "Please bless this food, Lord. Thank you for directing me to this lovely town, and for allowing me to help this very worthy woman. Amen."

Phil glanced up and saw tears shimmering in her eyes. What was it about his words that made her feel so emotional? Should he say something, or ignore it completely? He thought the latter far safer, especially since if he put his arms around Merry to comfort her, it might be his undoing.

"Eat up while it's hot."

She stared across the table at him, her mouth open, as if ready to speak, but instead she stuffed omelet into her mouth.

"It's good," she said between mouthfuls. "You should make this for the diner sometime."

Perhaps. It was a good staple item for lunch service. Many of the lunchtime patrons wanted something quick so they could get in and out in record time. That was especially true of store owners.

"I could add it to the menu for lunch tomorrow if you like. Provided we have plenty of eggs that is."

"I'm not sure, but I can get more from the mercantile."

They finished eating, and he broached the subject from earlier. "What did you want to ask me earlier?

Merry

You started to ask *Is there a way*. To do what exactly?"

"It's not possible, so forget it." She was determined in her decision not to expand, and no matter what he said, she refused to clarify what it was she'd wanted to know.

Phil studied her as he sipped his coffee. He was almost certain he knew the question – *Is there a way you can stay in Dewberry?* He dearly wanted to stay, but it wasn't feasible. He had made a promise to *Bert's Eating House*, and he never went back on his promises. He was a man of his word, and when that stagecoach came through on Tuesday, he'd be on it, no matter how much it pained him to do so.

His heart thudded. He'd had little chance to wander around town, but what he'd seen of it really impressed him. Everything he would ever need was right here on this small shopping strip. Including *Ma's Diner*. It was everything he'd ever dreamed of in a diner. He'd worked in several diners and restaurants, and this was the only one that made him feel as though he was right where he belonged. According to Merry, the diner had been transformed since he'd arrived. There were far more customers, and they were spending more. Of course, the meals he produced were not cheap; they were gourmet meals that cost more to produce and were priced accordingly. He knew from experience that patrons would pay for the high-quality food they craved and deserved.

He was teaching Merry all he could in the short time they had available, but it wouldn't be the same. Phil had years of training and practice. He couldn't expect Merry to learn everything in under a week. It was impossible.

"What are you thinking about?"

His thoughts were all over the place, and Phil knew he was in an untenable situation. He would prepare himself to leave in a matter of days. There was no other choice available to him. Over the next few days, he would cram as much into Merry's training as was humanly possible. That would ease his conscious about leaving her.

Only he knew it wouldn't. The situation was far more difficult than he ever envisaged was possible.

Chapter Five

Phil carefully added today's specials to the blackboard that was now a daily occurrence in the diner. Each morning after the breakfast service, Merry and Phil sat down and worked out the main meals for lunch and supper.

Some days it depended on what supplies were in the pantry, and others it relied completely on Phil's whim. Merry enjoyed finding out what he would make that day, then sat with him to work out the ingredient list. Her customers were overjoyed with this newfound version of *Ma's Kitchen*, and she had to admit, she felt the same.

Having the same menu most days had become tedious. With Phil there, her days had become far more exciting. To be honest, it wasn't only to do with the menus. Just being near him sent a sliver of excitement through her, and when he touched her inadvertently, electricity pulsed up and down her spine.

It was curious in her eyes, because Merry had never had this reaction to another person, and especially someone like Phil who seemed to be an itinerant worker, moving from place to place on a regular basis. She guessed it probably became rather boring after a while, and figured he would feel the same way here if he stayed. Just as well he had somewhere else to go. She needed someone who would feel grounded and stay put, not take off when his boredom level reached its peak.

She sighed.

"Everything all right?" Phil stared at her, as though trying to fathom her thoughts.

"Perfectly fine, thank you for asking."

"If you're happy with this menu for today, we can start the list of ingredients and work out what we need from the mercantile."

She reached across to pull the menu closer, and their hands touched. She closed her eyes as a shudder wracked her entire body.

"Merry? Are you sure you're all right?"

She opened her eyes to find him studying her. *What was she to say?* That his touch sent tendrils of excitement through her? That being close to him set her nerve endings on edge? Or perhaps she should admit she had fallen in love with the one person she could never have – because he had to leave town on Tuesday, never to return again.

She dearly wanted to say all that but couldn't. The moment she admitted her true feelings, things would change between them. Phil was happily oblivious to how she felt, and that had to be a good thing. They only had a few more days together, and then he would be nothing but a distant memory.

Only she knew that wasn't true. She would remember that kiss, no matter how fleeting it had been, for all the days of her life. Well, at least until the next Phil came along and swept her off her feet. Merry was still a young woman, albeit a spinster, and had many years left to find the man of her dreams.

It broke her heart to think she had already found that person, the one she believed to be her soulmate, but she was to lose him as quickly as he'd arrived.

"Are you sure you're fine? You seem to be far away." He had moved closer, far too close for comfort, and their faces were mere inches apart. He was so close she could feel his warm breath on her lips.

Merry swallowed. This was the last thing she wanted or needed. She reached for the glass of water sitting in front of her and drank it down greedily, trying to force herself back to reality. "Positive. Shall we go over the list of ingredients now?"

He stared at her curiously, then turned his attention toward the list sitting in front of them. The quicker they completed this task, the sooner she could leave the diner and get some fresh air. It might even clear her head enough to put some sense back into her thoughts.

Merry could only hope it worked.

Phil stood back and glanced over the diner. He had a grin on his face, and Merry knew he was admiring his handiwork. The diner was full to the brim, and the moment a table was emptied of customers, she cleaned and readied it for new customers. It didn't take long before it was filled. With Phil's additional menu items, such as pancakes, some with syrup, others with apples and cinnamon, many of their patrons were coming on a daily basis now. Previously, they might come once a week, or even less.

Having a renowned chef at *Ma's Kitchen* was paying for itself ten-fold. Sadly time was ticking over, and he'd be gone as quickly as he arrived. Merry had decided to make the best of it while she had him. If nothing else, the additional income would pay to update the tired looking diner. The kitchen in particular needed a makeover, especially if customers continued to come in droves as they did now.

But Merry knew once he left Dewberry, so would the customers, and she would be right back where she started. Oh, the diner was busy enough, but not as busy as it was now – nothing like it.

"That was delicious, Mr. Dalton." Mrs. Grayson always ensured she praised those who had made her happy. She also ensured a person knew if she'd made them the complete opposite. "I hear you are still leaving our little town on Tuesday. Silly man."

She wandered over to defend him. Mrs. Grayson could be brutal when she didn't get her way. "Phil has no choice, Mrs. Grayson. He had already accepted another position before he arrived here."

The town matchmaker studied Merry. She wiped her mouth with a napkin, then sipped her coffee. "I am aware of that fact, Miss Jensen. Surely things can be changed. Dewberry needs Mr. Dalton here. *You* need him here."

She wasn't sure how to answer that. If only things could be changed, Merry would be quite pleased. No, strike that, she'd be ecstatic. And on more than one level. "Apparently not. Phil has no choice but to fulfil his obligation in Hamilton."

"Harumph!" The older woman was more than a little put out by Merry's response. "We'll see about that!" She drank down the remainder of her coffee and made for the door. "Put breakfast on my account Merry." She then pushed a wad of money toward Merry and stormed toward the door.

Phil stared at Merry wide-eyed. "Mrs. Grayson seems to be on a mission. And what's with the money?"

"Oh, she's on a mission all right." She leaned closer. "She is the town matchmaker, don't forget. As for the money, it's to settle up her account. It's her way of doing things."

If Mrs. Grayson got her way, Merry would be very happy, but she didn't hold out hope.

With the diner cleared of customers, with Merry's assistance, Phil began preparing for today's meals. Their order had been placed at the mercantile and would be delivered soon. It was far too much for Merry to carry, and Phil was far too busy at this time of day to collect it.

What was really needed was a helping hand. Someone who knew what they were doing and was willing to do the hard work required. Only she'd been down that road before, and was lucky if they lasted a week or two. The restaurant business was brutal, and teenagers simply weren't interested. They wanted high pay for little work. Merry wanted someone who was willing to learn, and was willing to pay the going rate, or even a little more if they did the work. Alas it had not worked out to date.

"What time will the mercantile deliver that order? There are only a couple of dozen eggs here." Phil's voice brought her out of her thoughts. Merry realized she was doing a lot of that lately. His presence had given her a lot to think about.

"It should be here shortly." She glanced up as there was a knock at the door. "Speak of the devil." She hurried toward the door and unlocked it, holding the door wide open for the mercantile owner. "This is Henry," she told Phil. "He owns the mercantile. This is our chef, Phil Dalton."

"I'd shake your hand, but mine are rather full," he said, juggling the order.

"Here, let me help." Phil reached over and relieved Henry of some of the heavier items, then carried them into the kitchen where he put them on the countertop.

When his hands were finally free, Henry reached out and the two men shook hands. "I've heard a lot about you. You're certainly good for my business." The other man grinned.

"It's only short-term," Phil said hurriedly. "I'm leaving town on Tuesday." He sounded deflated, and Merry could tell the last thing he wanted was to leave.

"You can't find a way to stay? All my customers talk about now is your cooking, and the gourmet meals they can get at *Ma's Diner*. It's getting a bit stale," he said with a grin. At least he wasn't upset, but then, Henry wasn't like that. He was a happy-go-lucky kind of person, who would lift your spirits if you were feeling down.

"It's out of my hands, I'm afraid." Phil sighed then, and picked up a tray of eggs. "Sorry I can't stay and chat. The lunch crowd will be here soon, and I need to get started on these omelets."

"And I should get back. The missus is looking after the store alone. Nice to meet you." The pair shook hands again, and Merry knew had Phil been staying, they might have become the best of friends.

Merry walked to the door with Henry and they chatted on the way out. "He seems nice."

"He is," Merry said with regret. "I'll be sorry when he's gone." And she would be. How she would manage in the diner without him, she had no idea. How she would get over him, was another problem entirely.

Chapter Six

Saturday night rolled around, and Phil was both looking forward to it, and dreading it. The Dewberry church held a dance once every two months, and it happened to fall while he was still there.

It would be a welcomed break, and the diner would close a little earlier. Merry told him that since the dance was held so infrequently, the town folks all attended, and there was no point in staying open.

Even before the last customer was gone, they began the clean up, then left to prepare for the dance. Phil walked Merry home and promised to be back in thirty minutes to collect her. "Is that long enough?" he asked, unsure how long it took for women to prepare for such an outing.

"It is plenty of time," she said, but he wasn't convinced. She closed the door behind her, and Phil returned to the saloon to freshen up and change. It had been a very long time since he'd escorted anyone on a date. The thought made him pause. *Was this a date?* He shook his head. It wasn't a date, he was merely ensuring Merry arrived safely, and would escort her home again.

And perhaps they might actually dance while they were at the dance. That was the part he was dreading the most. It wasn't that he didn't want to dance with her; it was the complete opposite. The problem was, he knew once he held her in his arms, he would never want to let her go. Ever.

Phil stared at himself in the broken and mottled mirror. His slicked back hair was still wet, and his face shone with moisture. He leaned in closer as he fashioned his tie, then pulled on his jacket. He stared across at his tattered luggage, and was reminded he'd relocated far too many times. Everything he owned was in that worn out case, and it wasn't much. He loved his work, but hated the fact he was always on the move.

Would it be any different if he found a way to stay in Dewberry?

It wasn't like any other town he'd worked in, and that was because of Merry. She was the reason he wanted to stay – not *Ma's Diner*, and not the townsfolk. It was Merry.

She was his soulmate, and he had known it almost immediately. *But how did Merry feel about him?* She'd not given Phil any indication she had feelings for him, and that had held him back. Sure, he'd stolen a kiss, but it seemed to mean nothing to her. It was the complete opposite for Phil – it had meant *everything* to him. The moment their lips met, he knew. Touching her concreted his feelings, and his world had changed from that very moment.

His fingers somehow found their way to his lips. He could still feel her lips on his, and God only knew the pain it caused him. *How could he leave Dewberry and never see her again?* He silently prayed for God to guide him, to show him a way to stay. His heart was breaking and would never be the same again.

Phil sat on the edge of the bed and pulled on his boots. He'd polished those boots until they shined. He would look his best for Merry if it was the last thing he did. As he tied the laces, his thoughts were still on Merry, the love of his life. How would she feel in his arms, with her body close to his? He shook his head. Instead of fantasizing about it, he needed to collect her and accompany her to the dance. Then, and only then, would he know.

He stood outside her door and took deep breaths, then let them out again. He could do this, he really could. Phil knew tonight would be difficult but vowed to make the most of it. He had little more than two days left with her, and he wanted them to be special for them both. He'd met practically everyone in Dewberry through the diner, but meeting people at your place of business was different to knowing them socially.

For all he knew, Merry could be totally different away from the diner. It would remain to be seen. He straightened his shoulders and cracked his neck. Phil rubbed a hand over his clean shaven chin. He wasn't a man to wear cologne on a daily basis, but for a special occasion such as tonight, he splashed a little musk cologne on his face. He hoped Merry would like it, rather than the food smell he usually carried.

Finally he was ready and lifted his hand to knock on her door. His fist had barely touched the wood when the door opened. The vision before him took Phil's breath away. Instead of the gray and black skirts matched with a white shirt, as she wore to work, Merry wore a sapphire blue gown made of the finest material – silk if he wasn't mistaken. The embroidered bodice was superb. Her outfit was topped by a peacock jacket that matched perfectly.

Her hair had been pulled back and styled into a loose chignon, topped with an arrangement of feathers and silk flowers. She was perfect from her head to her toes. Not that he could see her toes, but if he could, Phil knew they also would be memorable.

"You look…stunning." Words almost failed him, but at a time like this, it was the last thing he needed.

"You scrub up pretty well yourself." Her eyes seemed to twinkle, but he knew it was the moonlight playing tricks on him.

"I do hope you have a warm coat to wear over your outfit. It's rather chilly out tonight."

She leaned to one side and scooped up her coat and gloves. "All accounted for." She smiled then, and a flutter worked its way through him. Did she purposely wear plain clothes for the diner? He'd never seen her wear her hair like this before either. She usually plaited it and pinned it up out of the way. He was seeing a whole new side of Merry tonight. Not that he was complaining. He adored the day-to-day Merry, but this one was a whole different woman.

She stepped out of her house, and Phil helped her into the coat, then she pulled on her gloves. He offered her his arm, and she hooked hers through it. Warmth exploded in him the moment she touched him, even if it was through her gloves and his jacket. He headed toward the church hall where the dance was being held, proud to have this woman on his arm.

As they got closer, Phil could hear the music. Sounds of laughter and talking permeated the air, and most of all happiness. When they arrived, joy surrounded them. Merry's face lit up as they walked inside, and it filled him with delight. To see her happy was his ultimate aim. *But how long for?*

The music stopped as they arrived. Phil led her to a chair, and they sat down, but only momentarily as the band soon began to play again. His heart pounding, Phil stood in front of her. "May I have this dance?"

Merry stood, and he took her hands. They moved to the crowded dance floor as his heart continued to pound. This was the moment he'd been dreading. Once he felt his arms around her, Phil knew things would never be the same again. And he was right. He would never forget that moment for as long as he lived. He held her hand and snaked his other arm around her waist. Merry did the same. The music was slow and romantic, just as he had envisaged. She glanced up into his face and smiled. She seemed to be enjoying herself, which pleased him.

And then it happened. She rested her head against his chest. He gently let go of her hand and brought his arm around her, until she was completely enveloped by him. Phil knew he could stay like this forever, and would be thrilled to never let her go. He felt Merry's arm come up around him, and was more contented than he had been for a very long time.

Without warning, the music stopped. His heart thudded. It meant he had to let her go. Instead he stood there, still with Merry wrapped in his arms. The last thing he wanted was to sit down, to lose that connection with her. The music suddenly began again, and they stayed right where they were.

It wasn't until the band took a break and refreshments were served that they left the dance floor. One thing was now cemented in Phil's mind – and that was he was totally and utterly in love with Merry. But he had no way to do anything about it.

"Last dance of the night." The announcement set his heart to racing. This would be the last time he would ever hold Merry in his arms; he needed to make the most of it.

"Shall we," he asked far more calmly than he felt as he took the mug of apple juice from her hands.

A sadness crossed her face, and Phil knew Merry had the same thought he'd had. It would be a sad few minutes as they danced together, but they needed to make the most of it. He took her by both hands, and led Merry back onto the dance floor. As the couples all took their places, the music began.

Slow and steady, and again, very romantic, setting the mood for the end of the dance night.

Phil lifted his arms and wrapped them around her, their bodies closed. She leaned her head against his chest, and he leaned in so they were almost cheek to cheek. The warmth he felt was more than just from skin to skin, as there was little of that. It was a deeper kind of warmth, one that you only got being near the person you loved.

All of a sudden Merry shifted. Her head was now back on his chest, and her arm slid down from around his back. He glanced down to see her wiping a tear from her face. He knew exactly how she felt – he didn't want this to end, but there was truly no way around it. He wiped away her tears, and whispered so only Merry could hear. "I love you with all my heart, and want to be with you for the rest of my days." She glanced up but didn't say a word. "I truly wish I could find a way to stay here." Her tears continued to fall, and he wiped them away again, his heart breaking a little more with every tear that fell.

"I love you too," she said softly, before resting her head against his chest again.

The music stopped and he glanced up to see Mrs. Grayson watching them carefully. She nodded her head; it was subtle, but Phil saw it. He wasn't sure what she wanted him to do – his future was set, and there was no way out of it.

He led Merry to the cloak room and collected her coat. Phil knew she wouldn't want to stay longer given her state of upset right now, and they began the short journey home. To end the night this way was heartbreaking, but they both knew he couldn't stay. They'd known it from the start.

Mrs. Grayson hurried over to the couple, and leaned in, speaking quietly. "Don't give up hope," she told them. "You never know what is around the corner." Almost the moment she finished speaking, she hastened to her carriage.

It left Phil wondering what she meant. But not for long. It had been a wonderful night, until it had become too much for them both. The weather had turned, and it was beginning to snow, he needed to get Merry home before she froze. He helped her into her warm coat, and she hooked her arm through his, and they headed home.

They'd only just turned the corner when the wind picked up, and the snow was suddenly heavier. He pulled her along as quickly as her short legs would carry her, and wrapped an arm around her, pulling her close. "The weather can be unpredictable here this close to Christmas," she said against the wind and the snow. She turned her collar up against the cold, and Phil wished he had a scarf to give to her.

Her teeth began to chatter, and he could have kicked himself. It wasn't terribly far from Merry's house, but in this weather the short trip was dreadful. He turned as he heard a carriage behind them. "Get in," Mrs. Grayson called from inside the carriage. Phil had no intention of refusing her kind offer.

"Thank you, Mrs. Grayson," he said, more concerned about Merry than himself. He reached over and brushed the snow from Merry's cheek. The older woman watched his every move, her gaze relentless.

"You are most welcome, Mr. Dalton. I couldn't have the pair of you freeze to death, could I? After all, we can't have a wedding if you're both dead." She said the words so matter-of-factly it shocked Phil. *What was the old lady playing at now?*

"We can't have a wedding," Merry said, her teeth still chattering. Phil slid closer to her and placed his arm around her again, endeavoring to warm her up.

"Ah, but you never know, do you?" Mrs. Grayson studied them both for a moment or two, then leaned back in the carriage, her arms crossed over her chest. Then she didn't say another word until they dropped Merry home. "Prepare yourself to stay, Mr. Dalton," she said firmly as they arrived outside the saloon.

"That is not possible," he said equally as firm. "Thank you for the ride. I appreciate it, and I know

Merry did too. The poor thing was chilled to the bone."

"Women are like that, but now she will have you to warm her up." She smiled that sly smile he'd seen a time or two over the past days but thought little of it. Even Mrs. Grayson couldn't change the arrangement he'd made with *Bert's Eating House*. It was absolutely impossible. They were relentless when securing an employee, and to date had never let an employee leave outside their agreed time. They weren't about to start now.

"Goodnight, Mr. Dalton. Sleep well." This time she grinned. Phil went inside the saloon, and when he glanced up again, the carriage was gone. He wondered what the old dear was up to. But he knew it would take a miracle for him to be able to stay in Dewberry.

Chapter Seven

Phil collected Merry for church the next morning, both of them knowing they were only prolonging the agony. After today, they had one more day together, and then they would be torn apart. Likely forever, because who knew what would happen between when Phil left and when he returned, if indeed he ever did return.

Merry's heart pounded at the thought of it all, and she had fought back tears the entire morning. Last night she'd cried herself to sleep. It would have been better if they'd never met.

She knew that was untrue – never would she want to miss the opportunity of meeting Phillip Dalton. He was a kind and gentle man who had extraordinary skills in the kitchen.

They were a perfect match, and they both knew it.

Merry

As they sat together in church, Merry couldn't concentrate. She barely heard a word the preacher said, and nothing sank into her extremely distracted mind. Phil was equally distracted as far as she could tell, and his face was strained instead of the usual softness it normally held. They sat with their arms still hooked, and every now and then, Phil patted her hand, as if trying to comfort her for what they were both to endure soon.

How could it be this hard? They had been complete strangers less than a week ago. But Merry knew the answer; God had placed Phil in her diner for a reason. They were soulmates, and were meant to be. Only divine intervention could save them now, but she knew that was impossible. Even if she prayed for the next two days straight, he would still have to leave Dewberry.

She turned her head away as tears began to fall again. The pain in her heart was overwhelming, and she suddenly fled the one place she'd always found comfort and refuge. Even her God could not help, but in His own way, He would help her through this.

She heard footsteps behind her, but continued, nonetheless. No one, not even Phil could bring her comfort now. With their future on a collision course, nothing and no one could help her, help them. Not even Mrs. Grayson who professed to be able to fix anything and everything.

Merry knew that wasn't the case this time.

As she wiped at her cheeks, Phil's arms came up around her. "You're not alone," he said quietly. "Our God is here supporting us both, now and into the future." He pulled her close and produced a handkerchief, which he handed to Merry. "We'll get through this."

"It feels like my heart has been wrenched out of my chest," she said between sobs, then rested her head on his chest. Phil's heart pounded as hers did, and she knew she wasn't alone in her anguish. It didn't pacify her, but made it even harder knowing he was hurting as much as she was.

They stood there together for what seemed an eternity, until Phil led her into the church hall where they had danced together the evening before. He made Merry a cup of tea, hoping that might calm her down, but it made little difference.

She knew it wouldn't work, even before he handed her the beverage. This was not something that could be fixed merely by drinking tea. Or coffee for that matter. Heartache was not a thing that could be cured with the snap of the fingers.

Normally, Merry would stay and mingle with the other parishioners, but not today. She must look a fright, and frankly, she was not in the mood to socialize, especially feeling the way she did. Who knew if she might start crying again while discussing something important?

They hurried away as church ended and the crowd surged out the door and toward the hall. "Miss Jensen, Mr. Dalton."

Mrs. Grayson's voice trailed behind them as they made their quick getaway. She was the last person Merry wanted to see right now. More likely than not, the woman would try to convince them everything would work out all right. Only Merry knew better, and was certain Phil felt the same.

Everything would not work out, and there was no way to make it happen. If nothing else, this fact was cemented in her mind. Not even the Good Lord Himself could fix this.

It was difficult to get privacy in Dewberry, so they headed to the diner. Sunday was the one day of the week *Ma's Diner* was closed. Instead of sitting opposite each other as they normally did, Phil squeezed up next to Merry, trying to console her.

Coffee in hand, she took a sip here and there, but was mostly uninterested. If he was honest, he felt the same. All he wanted to do was spend time with her. In less than forty-eight hours they would be separated, never to see each other again.

At least for a year. That was the arrangement he'd made with Bert's, and he didn't even have to ask them to know they would not let him out of that arrangement. Not even if he paid them to do it. *Bert's Eating House* were notorious when it came to their chefs. They were poached, stolen, and absolutely coveted. They did everything to keep their desired staff with them as long as possible. Had Phil known his life would change course in a tiny town in the middle of nowhere, he would never have agreed to work there. He adored Dewberry, but he especially adored Merry.

What if they married? Would Bert's let him off the hook? Phil knew without even asking they wouldn't. He would marry Merry in a flash, but what was the point if they were doomed to be apart for the next twelve months? He swallowed back the emotion as he realized their situation was utterly hopeless. Neither of them wanted to be apart, and he sure as heck didn't want to live in Hamilton while Merry was here in Dewberry.

He glanced up as he heard a knock on the door. Mrs. Grayson. She was the last person he wanted to see right now, but he went and opened the door anyway. It was the polite thing to do, even if it wasn't what either Merry or himself wanted. "Mrs. Grayson."

"Mr. Dalton." She scrutinized him then, and it made Phil uncomfortable. "You both left in such a hurry, before I could talk to you. I called out to you – didn't you hear me?" She studied him again. "I see."

Without him saying so much as a word, she'd guessed they'd ignored her. "Merry is inconsolable," he said quietly, so only the woman in front of him could hear. "We are having coffee if you wish to join us?" He locked the door before anyone else put it in their minds to join them.

She sat opposite Merry, and Phil wandered out to the kitchen to pour coffee for Mrs. Grayson, then took his place again. No one said a word for quite some time.

"You need to have faith," Mrs. Grayson said after she'd drank half her coffee. "The Good Lord works in mysterious ways." She smirked then and it annoyed Phil. They all knew there was no resolution to this problem. Nothing short of Bert's burning down would solve the issue. And the chance that would happen was less than one percent.

"The stagecoach leaves at eight Tuesday morning. We all know I will be on it."

She smirked again, and it was really beginning to irritate him.

Suddenly she reached over the table and covered Merry's hand. "Have faith," she said, then gulped down the remainder of her coffee, then began to leave. "Thank you for the coffee, Mr. Dalton," she said, then headed to the door. Phil followed and locked the door behind her. Merry had said the woman was curious, strange even, but her behavior today was downright bizarre.

He headed into the kitchen and made lunch for them both. It would be one of the last meals they shared, and he was absolutely dreading it.

Monday was horrendous. Not in the sense of the customers or the food, but both of them were downhearted and depressed about their untenable situation. Mrs. Grayson had not shown her face in the diner again, but Phil had seen her carriage, so he knew she was in town.

Everything she said indicated Mrs. Grayson had something up her sleeve. What it could be, Phil had no idea. Whatever it was, it had fallen through. The proof of that was in the fact he still had to leave Dewberry. If she'd been successful in whatever, they would have heard by now.

Further deflated, he wandered around and chatted with the customers. It would be his last opportunity, and he wanted to make the most of it. They all expressed how sad they were he was leaving, and couldn't he stay instead? Didn't they know he would if it was even remotely possible? It had to be blatantly obvious to anyone who saw them together that he was madly in love with Merry, and she with him. Although, when he thought about it, they did endeavor to maintain a professional appearance at the diner.

The supper service was the worst. It meant they only had a couple of hours left together at most. As though to torture them even more, they seemed to brush their hands every now and then. Phil was sure he'd heard Merry cry out at one point, but she denied it.

As he locked the door behind the last customer, he leaned against the door. They would clean up, and then he'd walk her home for the last time. He felt hollow, almost as though someone had died. It wasn't unlike losing a loved one to death, because he was losing Merry.

He'd vowed not to show his emotions to Merry and would stick by that promise to himself. He would be stoic, no matter what it took. At least he would appear to be that way, even if it was eating him up inside.

"I guess this is it," Merry said as she collected soiled dishes. "Why don't you go? It will make it easier on us both." She turned her head, and he knew she was on the verge of tears.

"I'm not leaving you with this mess." He collected a number of dishes himself and headed toward the kitchen.

Merry washed and he dried, totally in silence. They had talked this through a number of times, and always came to the same resolution – Phil had to leave. When everything was washed, dried, and put away, Phil made them a light supper. It had been their routine almost from the start. Merry poured the coffee, and he brought their food out to the diner. The few dishes this created would be quickly cleaned. He never allowed Merry to come into a mess in the morning.

"It's good," she said as she ate. Phil acknowledged her with a nod. It was nothing special, scrambled eggs with bacon, and a side of toast. There was still some leftover Blancmange, and they would have that for dessert. There was nothing worse than throwing out spoiled food.

The atmosphere between them was palpable, but neither said a word. Phil glanced up now and then to check if Mrs. Grayson had arrived. What ever the woman had going on, he thought they'd know by now. It was obviously not meant to be.

After they cleaned up from their supper, they cleaned the kitchen, then walked home together as they'd done each and every night since Phil arrived. It pained him to know Merry would walk alone from now on. In the dark and with no one to protect her. He knew he would think about her at this time every night and worry those young men had accosted her. It was more than he could bear.

When they arrived at her home, he unlocked the door as he'd done so many times before. Only tonight he took her in his arms and kissed her deeply. Snow fell against his back, covered his hair and ran down his back via his collar, but Phil didn't care. He wanted to spend every moment with Merry, before they were torn apart.

"I...I can't do this," she finally said, then pulled away. "I am going to miss you more than I ever thought possible." Tears ran down her face, and he wiped them away.

"I already miss you," he said quietly. "I love you more than words could ever say." Instead of answering, she suddenly stepped back and closed the door quickly, as though doing it fast would make the pain less.

Phil pulled his collar up around his neck and headed toward the saloon for the last time. He would pack his meagre belongings tonight, knowing he wouldn't sleep, and would be at the stage office early in the morning. As much as he wished he could, he couldn't afford to miss the stagecoach yet again.

Heavy snow fell, making it difficult for Phil to make his way to the stage office. He wasn't sure if it was the snow making his legs feel heavy, or the weight of the world on his shoulders. The stagecoach was already there when he arrived, and his heart plummeted. He carried his tattered luggage, and checked it in before waiting in the office area. It would be warmer there than on the stage, since they had a roaring fire going. There were two older women chatting as they waited, a young woman with a toddler on her knee, and a young couple who appeared to be newlyweds. The latter pulled at his heart strings. At least the trip wasn't to be overly long, so he wouldn't be tortured for days on end. No matter how long they stayed on the stagecoach, he knew the newlyweds would remind him of Merry and himself, and all he'd lost.

At his insistence, Merry agreed she wouldn't see him off. She had the diner to attend to, and neither of them needed the additional heartache. He thought it would make the morning easier, but now knew nothing would make this situation less difficult.

"All aboard." The call made his heart thud. This was really happening. Phil ushered the others aboard before himself, and saw they were comfortable before settling himself. His thick warm coat would come in handy later when the weather turned, so at least his legs would be warm. As if that was the least of his worries, but Phil was trying not to think about Merry.

It wasn't working.

He pictured her in the little diner, with her grey skirt, white shirt, and frilly apron over the top. She would be standing at the large stove preparing for the onslaught of breakfast customers. She would be scurrying from the kitchen to the diner, rushing to service all her hungry customers. The thought of it was enough to make a grown man cry. But Phil fought his emotions, and sat with his back straight, not allowing himself to break down.

"Yaaa!" The driver called for the horses to move, and they started with a jerk. His heart pounded, and a headache was beginning to form. *Could he have done more to ensure he stayed in Dewberry?* But Phil knew there was nothing to be done, and settled himself back on the hard seat, steeling himself for the long and tortuous trip ahead.

They'd been moving only a short time when the stagecoach stopped suddenly, almost tossing him off his seat. The young mother held tight to her child, and the newlyweds grabbed hold of each other.

The silence was intense – until the driver began to shout. "What are you doing, woman? Get out of the way!"

Phil stuck his head out the window to try and find out what the commotion was all about. There was a carriage was across the road, blocking their path. It seemed familiar. At second glance, Phil realized it was Mrs. Grayson's carriage! Her own driver sat resolute while his mistress shouted orders. "Stop the stage," she bellowed as she waved something in the air.

"What do you think you already did, you silly old fool!" The driver was none to happy, but Phil's heart pounded. *What was she up too?*

"I need to talk to one of the passengers," she demanded. He heard the driver curse but nonetheless he agreed.

Mrs. Grayson opened the door nearest Phil. The driver climbed down to see what all the fuss was about. "I got it!" she shouted as she waved the paper about.

On closer inspection, Phil noticed a telegram in her hand. She shoved it toward him. "Bert's is letting you go! It took quite some doing, and a lot of negotiations, but finally they agreed." Tears ran down the old lady's face. Phil didn't think he'd ever see the day. Nor did he believe what Mrs. Grayson told him.

He straightened out the partly crumpled paper and read the words for himself. *Bert's Eating House* were letting him out of his agreement. He didn't believe it at first and read the words yet again. Emotion threatened to overtake him. *How could this be true?* He had no idea what Mrs. Grayson had done or said to convince them, nor did he feel the need to know right now. He only cared about one thing – he could stay in Dewberry and be with the love of his life.

He climbed down and the driver unloaded his luggage, then turned to Phil. "Good luck, young fella," he said. "Now can we get goin'?" he asked Mrs. Grayson, beginning to sound agitated.

"You certainly can." Mrs. Grayson turned to Phil and hugged him. "Now go to your lady and give her the good news."

Despite the snow, he almost ran to the diner, his heart pounding the entire way. When he opened the door, Merry was heading to the kitchen. She turned to face him, then ran into his arms, tears streaming down her face. Phil knew he'd come home, and would never leave, not without Merry.

Epilogue

Three years later…

Phil watched his young apprentice put the final touches on the Summer Pudding, which he served all year round, summer or not, and felt pleased with himself. Bringing Daniel Taylor to work at the diner had been one of his best ideas.

The now twenty-year-old had also lost his job when *Joe's Eatery* had burned to the ground, and had still been without a job. After all, who would employ an apprentice chef with only a few months under his belt? Why Phil hadn't thought of it far earlier, he didn't know, but it provided the assistance he and Merry needed. Even more so now. He was coming along nicely, and was close to the end of his apprenticeship. During the quieter times, he was able to give the young man his undivided attention.

It might afford Phil the opportunity to take days off from the diner and spend more time with his family.

At the same time he'd offered the position to Daniel, he'd also offered Annabelle Carson the opportunity to work at the diner. She was the best server they'd had at Joe's, and the customers adored her. They could certainly do with her help.

With Christmas creeping up on them, *Ma's Diner* was busier than ever. With Phil as their permanent chef, it helped to bring the customers to them. Merry didn't mind as much as he thought she would, especially given the circumstances.

"You've been summoned," Annabelle said as she rolled her eyes.

Phil sighed. "Again?"

"Again. I don't think Mrs. Grayson will ever let you forget exactly who negotiated for you to stay in Dewberry and not have to fulfil your agreement with Bert's."

Now it was Phil's turn to roll his eyes. He added a sigh for good measure. "Plate up one of those mini Christmas Puddings please, Daniel. We'll make this old lady happy yet." He grinned and wiped his hands down his apron. Not that they were grubby, but it wouldn't do to have enough a skerrick of flour on his hands.

He walked toward the old lady's table, fully aware of her eyes on him. "Mrs. Grayson," he said, placing the Christmas Pudding and jug of custard in front of her. "Compliments of the house. Did you enjoy the Roasted Goose?"

"I did indeed. My compliments to the chef." She smiled then, and he felt relieved. She might have arranged for him to be with the love of his life, but she was still their most difficult customer, even if she was like part of the family.

She adored his food, and Phil knew she did, but he still held his breath every time he asked. Mrs. Grayson would surely tell him if she didn't like his food. Not that it had happened yet.

She glanced around then. "Merry not here today?"

"As much as she loves it here, she needs her rest."

Moments later, the door to the diner opened, and Phil glanced up. "Papa!" Little legs slowed down their toddler son as he headed toward his father.

Phil leaned down and swooped the boy up into his arms. "James," he said quietly. "I missed you. I'm glad you could come and visit." The one-year-old put his arms around Phil's neck and hugged him tight. Warmth filled him, and Phil smiled. Merry followed behind and finally caught up.

"Sit down, my dear," Mrs. Grayson said, a smile on her face. "You must be exhausted." Merry slid onto the seat opposite the woman. "How long to go now?"

"Not long at all. A few weeks at most." She put a hand to her belly. "He's having a good old kick right now." Phil moved in with their son and placed his little hand on his mother's belly.

"That's your brother or sister," he told the boy. Not that he really understood at his age. Phil studied James as his eyes opened wide in amazement.

He silently said a prayer of thanks to God for bringing him to Dewberry, and for ensuring fate prevailed. He had been fulfilled the day he met Merry, and would be forever grateful for his little family, that God-willing, would continue to grow.

The End

From the Author

Thank you so much for reading my book – I hope you enjoyed it.

I would greatly appreciate you leaving a review where you purchased, even if it is only a one-liner. It helps to have my books more visible!

Books in this series:

Book One – Ivy
Book Two – Holly
Book Three – Noelle
Book Four – Belle
Book Five – Merry

About the Author

Multi-published, award-winning and bestselling author Cheryl Wright, former secretary, debt collector, account manager, writing coach, and shopping tour hostess, loves reading.

She writes both historical and contemporary western romance, as well as romantic suspense.

She lives in Melbourne, Australia, and is married with two adult children and has six grandchildren. When she's not writing, she can be found in her craft room making greeting cards.

Links:

Website: *http://www.cheryl-wright.com/*

Blog: *http://romance-authors.com/*

Facebook Reader Group:
https://www.facebook.com/groups/cherylwrightaut hor/

Join My Newsletter:

https://cheryl-wright.com/newsletter/